PARANORMAL ROMANCE#2

Compiled & Edited by

D. Kershaw | Maggie Pawsey | S.N. Graves

Also available and coming soon from Black Hare Press

DARK DRABBLES ANTHOLOGIES

WORLDS	APOCALYPSE
ANGELS	LOVE
MONSTERS	HATE
BEYOND	OCEANS
UNRAVEL	ANCIENTS

BHP WRITERS' GROUP SPECIAL EDITIONS

STORMING AREA 51

EERIE CHRISTMAS

BAD ROMANCE

TWENTY TWENTY

OTHER VOLUMES

DEEP SPACE

WHAT IF?

KEY TO THE KINGDOM

DEEP SEA

BEYOND THE REALM

Twitter: @BlackHarePress

Facebook: BlackHarePress

Website: www.BlackHarePress.com

TABLE OF CONTENTS

HOUSE BEATS

By Raven Corinn Carluk

I slammed back the shot of vodka and leaned into the wave of intoxication. Delightful and tingling and following the previous three drinks right to my head. Between the MDMA and the alcohol, I was riding high and more than ready to do my thing.

Several strangers took my place when I moved away from the bar. It felt like more people wanted to drink than dance, but that was only in the immediate vicinity. As soon as I neared the dance floor, I was swept into the frenetic tide, to the sea of gyrating bodies.

I rubbed against men and women as I passed, a goddess in leather, silver, and crystals. My outfit was provocative without being revealing, seeking attention without being an invitation. I basked beneath their gazes, the seven crystals I wore drawing in their energy.

A ritual as large as I planned would require as much power as I could get, and this nightclub had more than enough to spare.

I let the bass line take me, let the

intoxication guide my motions. We were all one mass, moving and bobbing and rubbing. The heat of lust and life surrounded me, pressing against my soul. A groan escaped me, swallowed by the rising tempo, and I ground against the closest dancer. Would that I needed this for every ritual.

Sexual energy fed my crystals. One of each chakra, each larger than my thumb, they throbbed with the music and the crowd. Cold against my pulse points and in my cleavage, they started to heat with the influx of energy.

A presence touched mine. Not the man I gyrated with, but someone close. Definitely male, all sorcerous power and pride. A perfect balance to an earthly witch like myself.

I opened my eyes, looking for the man in question. Strobing lights confused my vision, but I felt him with every fibre of my being. Close. Getting closer. Tingles raced up my spine, and an ache built in my core. I needed him, as I hoped he needed me too.

Firm hands settled on my shoulders, like a storm settling on a mountain. Commanding, primal, raw. Dark to my light. Strong to my soft. Wild to my control. Aching to spill to my eagerness to absorb.

God to my Goddess.

I leaned back with a sigh, relishing his touch. His hands remained on my shoulders and he held absolutely still as I writhed against him. We were of a height, so all appropriate curves found all the correct angles. I happily pressed myself to him, relishing his heart.

The song changed, becoming hard, driving, with more bass than anything else. I groaned, dropping my head back on his shoulder, and lifted my hands. Sensuality and intoxication took over, leading me through a ritual older than time.

He followed the command of the music, began his dance. Hands travelled up one side of my arms, then back down the other. His touch continued along my breasts, my sides, my hips. His lips brushed my ear as his power wrapped around me, heavier than the music guiding us.

We fell into the rhythm, began to move as one. The crowd became only another source of power for the two of us. I harnessed the power around us, feeding and opening, while he forged and drove and built. The ancient dance of man and woman, of priestess and priest.

Too long since I'd worked with a man. The sensation of those energies had become a memory, but my silent partner reminded me with every touch and flex and thrust. He gave; I took. He offered; I accepted.

Pressure and power and pleasure built as we followed the commands of nature. We were balance and opposition, duality and singularity. I moaned as wanton release loomed, the crescendo of the song matching my own impending climax.

He sensed the cresting wave and took control. Hands gripped tighter on my hips, keeping my body close to his. Grind and thrust and echoed groans as the beat pounded on and on.

The song peaked and broke, carrying me with it. I cried out, but the sound was lost in the music as my knees buckled. Firm hands and steady strength kept me from collapsing as waves of magic and ecstasy washed through, over, and around me. Energetic gateways opened, carrying myself and my partner to higher awareness.

Dizzy and breathless, I was barely aware of him moving us from the dance floor. Stars danced behind my eyes, and the thunder of my heart drowned out the next song that started. Power swam through me, pinging against my chakras, filling my crystals to over-full. Sparks and tingles ignited every nerve as my over-sensitive body attempted to compensate.

His mouth brushed my ear, sweet nothings that grounded me once more, pulled me back from the chaos of post-climax. Seconds, minutes, years passed as I came back to myself, allowing him to take me from the dance floor to somewhere more peaceful.

"Feeling better?" he asked, rich voice rumbling in my head, barely louder than the music. Even in a back hall, the beats dominated all conversations.

"Mhm." I couldn't manage anything else, still riding a tide of magic and intoxication. My head swam, and I really just wanted to bask in the afterglow.

"Same time next blue moon?" His arms held me close, comforting and strong.

"Mmhmm," I purred. I wished I could do this more often, but I couldn't risk losing this kind of interaction. My High Priest would ruin me otherwise. A sweet poison and temptation that would steal my focus from my work. I couldn't indulge in this man all the time and still be a competent High Priestess.

With a kiss on the nape of my neck, he took his leave.

CATCHING FIRE
By Amber M. Simpson

The gasoline can is heavy in my hands as I lug it into the abandoned house on Scott Street. No one's lived here since I was a little girl. My best friend and I used to sneak in and bum cigarettes from the squatters who sought refuge within these walls.

It's the perfect place for what I need to do.

Wading through a sea of broken beer bottles and discarded drug paraphernalia, I make my way to a room in the back. An old piss-stained mattress lies half hidden beneath a mound of fetid trash.

I pop off the gas cap and douse the bed with a generous amount of its contents. The strong, heady odour of gasoline invades my nostrils and I suck it in greedily. I feel the pull of the tough, leathery skin around my mouth as a smile stretches my face. Giddy with excitement, I twirl in circles, the sharp fumes intoxicating.

It's been six months since I last saw him in the fire that ravaged my flesh. Six long months of lying in the hospital, dreaming of his fiery touch.

From my pocket come the matches, and with one smooth strike, I light three. Tossing them on the bed, I'm at once rewarded with a large whoosh of heat as it ignites.

My heart pounds with anticipation as the fire expands, crawling across the mouldy floor. It licks the legs of a rickety armoire, likes the taste, and devours it. Leaping flames caress the walls, leaving sooty black kisses behind.

Feasting hungrily, smoke fills the room, burning my throat and lungs. My stinging eyes scan the flames in desperate search of the Fire Man.

In my hospital delirium, I cried for him often, the man I had summoned with the strike of a match. I had tried so long, setting fire after fire, with nothing to show for it but smoke. It was when I learned the secret that he finally showed himself to me—when I offered myself to the flames I created. I had to let myself burn.

Now, the fire roars before me, and I drop to my knees, coughing on acrid smoke. Outside, I hear the dreaded wail of sirens in the street.

No! They can't take him away from me again! They won't!

I look about wildly, gasping for breath, and—*there!*—I see him, taking shape. He materialises slowly—tall, muscular body shifting with the movement of flame. His eyes burn red like two hot coals, while flames flicker on his head in place of hair.

Spellbound, I watch as his naked form solidifies. Fiery. Bright. Magnificent.

I climb to my feet, and like the Red

Sea, the fire parts between us. He opens his arms and I run and leap, the flames quickly crowding us in. My sizzling skin smokes beneath his touch while his lava tongue melts my lips. Clinging to him, my body sparks, then rapidly ignites—and together we merge into a single bright flame and disappear into the fire.

First published, *Best of 2019 anthology*, Iron Faerie Publishing, 2020

SHATTERED LOVE
By Andrew Kurtz

Please do not judge me harshly because I murdered the man that I love.

I see the way you are rolling your eyes, but you must believe that I had good intentions.

Is it wrong for two lovers to want to be together for eternity?

When he offered to drink my blood and turn me into a vampire, I was ecstatic.

When his fangs pierced my flesh, I was overcome with emotions never experienced before.

When he turned to dust, I felt I should have warned him that the garlic I ate during the day was still in my bloodstream.

THE WIDOWER
By Chisto Healy

His name was Jack. Elena watched him from afar, as she always did. He was drinking a dry martini and watching television. She ached to sit beside him, to watch with him, to rest her head on his shoulder, but she couldn't. It was too big of a risk. She had to keep her distance.

Jack knew too much about her world. He plunged into it head first on a regular basis. It was what kept him going. She could sit beside the ordinary person, cuddle with them even and they would be none the wiser. They would never notice anything more than a sudden drop in temperature; nothing a blanket wouldn't fix.

Jack would know what the climate change meant though. He would check for other signs. He would get anxious. Then he would discover her, and it would break his heart. It would tear him to ribbons to encounter a spirit in his home only to find out it wasn't his wife.

Diane was Jack's existence. She was his world, and that world was ripped away tragically. It broke him down and ruined him. Elena watched it happen. Then just the same as it took him to his knees, his love for Diane brought him back from the ashes. The fire of hope, the determination to make it right, the tunnel vision that only true love could supply; it drove him onward.

Elena's heart broke for him. She wished that she could take his pain away, that she had that kind of power. She wished that he knew how much she loved him, how much she enjoyed spending her moments watching him and taking care of him. She wished that he could love her in return and allow the pain of his loss to subside over time. She would help him if he would let her, but she knew that he wouldn't. He would never let anyone in, alive or dead. His heart was solely designated for Diane and that was the end of his story. Sadly, Elena loved him more for it.

How could you not love someone that was so hopelessly devoted to someone? What in the world was more romantic than that? His quest to recover Diane from the ghoul that had taken her consumed his mind. He couldn't focus on the little things. Elena couldn't allow him to see her, to know that she lived with him, but she could show her love to him in other ways. She did her best to take care of him. She turned off the oven when he left it on. She started the coffee he made and forgot to turn on. She put his shoes where he could find them because he would look all over if she didn't, his mind swimming through the tide of grief. She did her best to keep the house clean without overdoing it and alerting him to her presence.

It had been almost two years since that

day, the day that took Diane from him and brought Elena into his life. It was the worst day of his life and the best day of hers, despite the fact that her mortal life ended long ago.

Jack was very close to his mother. It hit him hard when she took ill. It hit him harder when western medicine failed her and said there was nothing more to be done. He was willing to try anything as she laid there in his house, fading to nothing, and Diane was supportive of him the entire way. She never told him to stop, never told him he had gone too far. She stood by him through it all.

Then, his magical efforts to heal his dying mother opened a door, a door to the other side. It was only open for a moment, but that moment was long enough for a ghoul to grab Diane and pull her through. Jack screamed and tried to hold the door, to reopen it when it closed. He never noticed Elena slipping through in the commotion. In the end, the door was gone, Diane was gone, and Jack's mother succumbed to the illness and went to the other side anyway.

Elena knew that, in all his grief, Jack would see her as the enemy, so she remained hidden. She lived in the background. As the days passed, she grew to know him more and more and to care for him just the same. He delved deeper into the same terrible things that got his wife taken from him in his efforts to bring her back. Elena found it hard to watch sometimes, and she worried for his well-being and health. Sometimes she waited until he slept, and then seized the opportunity to come close to him, to stroke his face or kiss his forehead, whisper that she loved him.

At this point, she loved him so much that she wished he would find Diane and have his old life back. She just wanted to see him happy, even if it was with somebody else. Elena would have willingly given her freedom away and gone back through the gate to the other side if it would have brought Diane back to him.

Today was the day that she would be given the chance to make good on that. After two years of research and magic, Jack finally reopened the door. It was horribly dangerous and something as bad or worse as what came through last time could come through it again.

Elena knew that it wouldn't stay open

long enough for Jack to find his wife anyway, just as she knew that Diane wasn't just going to walk back out into reality. A ghoul had her and ghouls were power driven. It would keep her, enslave her. It wouldn't give her up without something in return. Ghouls could be beaten. Diane could escape. Even if she did though, she wouldn't know the way home. Elena on the other hand could travel that plane as she pleased, stay for as long as she wanted, and after all her time here, she knew how to contact Jack as well.

She hated the idea of going back but she knew what she had to do. She owed it to him. He was the one that gave her the freedom she had been enjoying for the past two years. It was more than that though. She loved him. She loved him with her whole heart and there was no greater way to show it.

When the door opened, Elena brushed her fingers over his face, slipped through it and shut it behind her. Jack was stunned by her touch at first, confused. Then it hit him that the door had slammed shut so soon after he got it open.

She could feel the surge of Jack's grief. It hit her like a shockwave. She couldn't hear him from where she now was, but she knew from the feeling, the vibration that rocked her, that he was screaming. The pull of his pain tugged at her heart, but she couldn't re-open the door. It was to keep him safe. She just whispered an apology he couldn't hear.

Elena could feel the warmth of the mortal world get sucked away like she was in a vacuum. She hugged herself against the sudden cold as she looked around at the others, the lost and lonely, floating by as if they were pulled by a current, stuck in a whirlpool of unresolved feelings. She remembered being one of them. For so long, before she met Jack, this was her existence. She was aimlessly wandering, aching for a life that wasn't hers anymore, heartbroken and alone.

Even if she had to return to this place, return to the flock, it would be different this time. She had two years with Jack. She had time to live in the light and warmth of the mortal world, a place where she was the cold, the intrusion. She had the time to fall in love and to feel it grow and blossom like a blooming flower. Even this place couldn't take that away from her. She would keep it in her heart forever.

Elena moved through the bodies in search of Diane or the ghoul that had taken her. She kept a wary eye for any other ghouls or threats that lurked in the shadows. There were many. Normally their hunger was for mortals and the apparitions coexisted, but they got restless at times without something to play with, and when they got restless ghouls got volatile.

She didn't see Diane, but she could see her trail, the embers of her humanity dripping like flames in the darkness. It was life, life that wasn't accustomed to this place. It bled out over time and the blood of life was light. After two years of being here, two years in the hands of a ghoul, Elena feared what she would find when she got to Diane. Looking around at the blank faces and empty eyes of the lost, she felt like she knew her answer. Her heart broke for the man she loved, and she voiced another apology he couldn't hear.

Then she found what she was looking for, a twisted, gnarled long-dead grey flaking tree—a ghoul tree. Diane was splayed across its front in a white gown, her limbs tied tightly to the sprawling branches. She was waif thin, her eyes sunken deep into her face, her cheekbones jutting out, and her flesh so pale and mottled grey, so similar to the tree she was tied to.

Elena could still retain the mental picture of Diane from the day they traded places. The woman had been full figured and voluptuous. Her hair that was now wisps of white, had been a deep chestnut.

Her olive skin had glowed. It was hard to believe this was the same woman, and yet Elena thought it well to find her as she did. The ghoul was draining her slowly, savouring it. She expected worse.

Then he was there. He descended upside down from the tree, hairless and sickly, smiling at her with wickedly yellow teeth. "I'm returning her," Elena said firmly. "You can have me instead."

"You are long dead," the creature hissed. "I eat life."

Elena nodded. "I have spent years in the mortal plane. I have embers of life to drain, memories of love and happiness to steal."

The ghoul seemed to think on it. "It doesn't taste the same," he spat. "How about I make you a deal? You let me have her, and I will use my magic to let you take her likeness. Then you can return as her…or more, her ghost."

Elena was silent. She stared into the ghoul's eyes. She knew that he would keep his word. She understood how these creatures worked. She was just stuck for an answer. It would be so wonderful to live with Jack, to be the one to receive his love and affection, to be able to be seen. It would be good for him as well, to have her back, looking healthy and beautiful as she had, even if she were a ghost.

Then again, it would be a lie and if she loved him, that would be a betrayal. He would probably prefer to have his withered, dying shell of a wife over an impostor that wore her beauty.

The ghoul was waiting for his answer.

She didn't know what to do. She knew how much Jack loved Diane. She also knew how much she loved Jack. Was it wrong to be selfish for love? She bit her lip. She looked over the withering Diane. Then she looked at the ghoul, and she nodded.

"I've made my decision," she said in the name of love.

LOVED BEYOND MEASURE

By Chris Bannor

Jacob felt the call of the water, like a lover whispering endearments against his skin. The dark of night didn't bother him as he walked across the beach, on a long-deserted stretch. He parked his car far enough away not to draw eyes to where he really went.

He was alone with this ache in his bones and the burning of his blood. The salt in the air was like a drug and he stripped off his jacket to feel it against his bare arms. He kicked out of his boots and left them behind in the sand. He felt lighter, and the waves beckoned.

He made it to the edge of the tidal pool, the dig of sharp-edged rock and shell under his feet, but he didn't care.

"I was afraid you wouldn't come."

He was beautiful. He wasn't quite human—his smile a bit too wide, his eyes too bright in the moonlight, his skin glimmered under the light of stars and moon in a way that no human's skin ever had.

"Parking was a bitch," Jacob tried to

keep the conversation light, to hide the need in his voice, but there was no denying his pull to the other.

"Were you scared?"

Jacob didn't answer the question but asked his own. "What's your name?"

"What?" he was taken aback, and Jacob understood why. His kind didn't give names lightly.

"You want me to trust you. To run off with you, away from everything I have ever known. And I'm here, but you have to give me something. Not a nickname, but the real thing."

Jacob took a step closer and raised his hand. The creature's pale skin disappeared underneath Jacob's dark skin in the moonlight and it entranced him for a moment before Jacob looked back into his eyes.

"Arran," the other said. "My actual name is Arran. No one has called me that…in an exceptionally long time."

"You enchanted me. Are you worried that I'll hurt you with your name?"

Arran raised his hand and caressed his cheek with the back of his fingers. "You don't need my name to hurt me. If you ever left, it would devastate me."

"Is that why you want to take me away from all this?" Jacob asked.

"Yes," Arran breathed the words against his lips. "We fae are territorial. I have my beautiful island and I have spent centuries looking for you, waiting for you to hear my call and find me."

"I would never leave you."

"Then come with me, now. Let me take

you away. I would never keep you there if you wanted to leave, but I can give you everything you have ever wanted. Just be mine."

"I am yours," Jacob answered. "Take me away, fae. I will follow wherever you go."

Arran pulled him into his arms and kissed him softly. "My Sidhe awaits."

Jacob closed his eyes and blackness pulled at his consciousness, but he wasn't afraid. Arran held him tight in his arms, whispering words of love as the world faded. Magic filled him, lifted him, turned him into something he could never be otherwise.

When he opened his eyes again, he was no longer quite human, but he was still loved beyond measure.

CLOSURE RITUAL
By D.J. Elton

I see a triangular effect of the ocean, moon, and intense emotion.

Let's sever all impressions of him from me. I ache and feel alone. At midnight I lie down on the sand in a white, death dress. Seawater runs along my feet to hair; the tides soak and immerse me. I sweat inwardly, feel ice cold externally.

The Indian Ocean—mighty sea itself—gently rips through my heart, extracting a pinched nerve. It is his grip, his festering memory.

My body, being part water, reacts well to this ritual. Then I want to drink milk, go home. Task completed.

WAIT

By David Green

I died before I turned twenty-one. Shinji stayed by my side as the illness burned me away like a scrap of paper caught by flames.

We were still in our honeymoon period when I fell sick. Through the pain and delirium, Shinji stayed strong, holding my hand when fever gripped me, keeping me fed and as comfortable as he could. Moments with him mix in the haze of that wasting disease, but I remember his last words to me, before my body gave in.

"Kazuno, please don't leave."

A magnificent white tunnel met me when I left my body behind. I felt its pull, heard its sweet music calling me home. I resisted. Tears streamed from my eyes as I turned away from the light. Instead, I focused on Shinji. My heartbroken husband, bent over my empty shell, despair and loneliness in his eyes.

He asked me not to leave, so I didn't. I waited for him.

I whispered words of consolation as he mourned my death. My sickness made me focus inwards, and I hadn't understood the effect it had on him. His face had aged, and grey appeared at the temples of his black, silken hair. I ached to touch him again, to tell him I loved him. That I waited.

If I shouted loud enough, he seemed to notice in subtle ways, like his mind decided he should act a certain way, when it was I who nudged him in these directions. Shinji deserved to be happy, and I tried to guide him towards it.

Five years after I died, he met Hatsumi. He resisted her at first, but I urged him to accept this beautiful beginning. I watched as they married. I cried tears of joy when their first child arrived.

I sat by his side through the divorce.

Hatsumi loved him but accused Shinji of not giving enough of himself to her. He agreed, and I knew why. Inside, he waited for me despite thinking he'd never see me again. How could he know different?

Now in his middle years, I witnessed Shinji loneliness. Each week he would leave flowers on my grave, a ritual he'd started after my burial and one continued through his marriage to Hatsumi. A pilgrimage she never understood. I peered over his shoulder when he would flick through decades old photographs of us. I'd try to wipe the tears from his face when they rolled down his cheek.

He's grown old, and his body declines. I'm with him as he rests in his hospital bed, his son and daughter asleep on the sofa, their heads against each other. They have their own families now. He watches them as his heart beats slower, a faint smile on his face. I wish Shinji's life had been better, but his children love him. He turns away and stares at the ceiling, eyelids drooping as the time nears.

"Kazuno," he whispers.

"I'm here," I reply in his ear. "I never left."

Shinji's eyes widen and he smiles as his heart beats for a final time. I take his hand, able to touch him for the first time in sixty years. I pull him to his feet.

He stands before me as a young man again, the white light behind me twinkling in his eyes. Shinji steps close and kisses me. I taste our happiness on my lips as our tears mingle there, his palm is firm against my cheek as he caresses my face.

"You waited for me?" he asks, pulling his mouth away and looking over my shoulder at the brilliant flare beckoning to him. I remember the wrench when I ignored it.

"A lifetime," I reply, taking his hand and turning towards the light. "Shall we go together?"

Shinji glances one last time at his sleeping children, a contented smile on his lips.

"Yes," he answers, squeezing my hand. It feels good.

Excitement flutters in my chest as we walk into the bright tunnel. It's been worth waiting for.

SMOKE SIGNALS

By Drew Starling

Today marks four cycles of the sun since the war ended, since I lost you.

Some days, I feel the weight of the decades in my frail bones.

Others, I forget you're gone at all and feel your warmth by my side when I wake.

It is you, isn't it?

I often think about how you would react to our world now.

The machines have fully taken over, but it's not as bad as it sounds.

We've learned to adapt, and they've allowed us to live.

You'd hate it.

Last night, I walked slowly through the old Silver District.

Remember the raucous gin joints and clubs we used to love?

The machines tore them down and filled the spaces with more memory banks.

I don't even remember their names.

But I remember the night we danced until dawn on the veranda.

LOCKDOWN PNR #2

You'd had too much to drink, and I'd never been in love before.

We knew what was coming for us, but just for a moment, we didn't care.

You were right... over... there.

All that remains of the world you knew is the sky.

It's the only thing that looks the same as it did back then.

It's the only place they haven't taken and covered in black.

But they will soon.

Until then, the sun still shines, and the stars still sparkle at night.

Sometimes, I look at the clouds, and I think I see you, sending me smoke signals.

It's not the world you fought for, it's

not the world you died for.

But it'll do until I see you again.

THE BROKEN VOW
By Galina Trefil

"I'm cold," whispered the dark mist hovering above the bed. "Let me in."

Lana swallowed. How could she refuse her own husband? Her hand shaking, she pulled back the blankets beside her. The featureless blackness drifted forward, settling in. "Cover me up," he hissed. "I can't do it myself."

"But…how?" He was only an entity, without a body to cover.

"Please, Lana," he murmured. Closer and closer, he crept against her, stealing her warmth.

When she spoke again, her anxious breath danced before her face. "'Till death do us part, remember?"

"I do. But, Lana, I'm not ready to leave."

DEMON LOVER

By Jacqueline Moran Meyer

A beautiful demon sat at a table sipping her soy-latte. A handsome stranger with a dishonest face sat beside her. He fell in love with her and confided every sin he committed—abusing women, abandoning his children, and stealing clients' life savings. He sometimes caught glimmers of her true ugly demon form. He didn't care. No one loved him like she did. When the Demon knew she'd won his undying devotion, she spat at him, screaming he deserved death, not love. She laughed when he swallowed the bottle of pills in his despair, then collected her reward from the Evil One.

First published, *101 Words*, 2019

THE BARGAIN
By Kimberly Rei

"She can read my mind, Steph."

My best friend laughed, the phone delivering her mirth directly, "No, she can't. I know you're addicted to her, but she's not actually magical."

Stephanie hadn't approved of Tianna from the beginning, but it was a best friend's job to be a pain in the ass. But there were things she didn't know. Things she couldn't know. Things Tianna *always* knew and shouldn't. Couldn't.

Our conversation moved on. I wasn't in the mood for her gentle disdain. This wasn't a whim, and I hadn't lost my wits. But I knew I sounded crazy. Hell, most days I felt crazy.

Tianna had spun into my world on a maelstrom of charm. I was jogging; she crashed into me on her bike. I thought I'd broken my wrist. Just an average girl-meets-girl tale. There was nothing but pain and shock for the first few moments, but when she helped me stand up, she cradled my wrist and bent her head down. I was too busy staring at the back of her white pixie-cut hair to notice what she was doing until she blew lightly over my skin. I jumped, she laughed, and the pain was gone.

"Just a scratch, love. Nothing to fret over."

She looked up, and I was lost. Eyes the colour of an ocean storm. Even as I smiled, they changed shade. The sun, or the clouds passing overhead, I told myself. So many things can shift eye colour. But hers were never still. Never calm. I was accepting her invitation to dinner before I registered she'd asked.

It's an old joke that a proper lesbian second date involves a moving van and new dishes. We weren't far off. Three months after we met, she moved into my home. It just made sense. Her place was tiny and in a questionable part of town. I had inherited a cottage from my grandmother, complete with adorable yard and fenced off garden.

Tianna was tending flowers as I chatted with Stephanie. I watched her through the kitchen window, my heart flipping over and my belly tightening. Love. Desire. I couldn't so much as think of her without both cresting. Steph was talking about job frustrations, but her voice had become a steady drone. Two years with Tianna hadn't eased anything. I dreamt of her. I ached for her. I would have given up food and drink for her, I was so sure her love would sustain me.

The last few months had pulled away the edges of the rosy overlay. I still couldn't look at her without wavering, but in quiet, private moments, I found clarity. And with that came questions that I couldn't answer. What did Tianna do when I was away? Did she have a family? A past of any kind? Surely we had discussed these things at some point, but I couldn't remember any of it.

I had once accused her of having an affair. She gave me that knee-buckling smile and told me I had nothing to worry about. I wasn't going anywhere. Even then, I wasn't overly comforted, but instinct and the shift of her eyes to storm grey had sealed my lips. One kiss and I couldn't fathom why I was upset with her.

Stephanie was repeating my name. I blinked and winced, "I'm so sorry!"

"Staring at Tia again?" The disdain was less gentle this time.

"No! No, of course not. Trying to read the expiration date on this creamer. I think it was around our high school graduation."

She didn't buy it, but she let me off the hook and shortly after, off the phone.

Tianna leaned in the kitchen doorway, "How's Steph?"

I steadied myself, refusing to look at her. Everything coiled with the need to curl into her and let that voice melt all worries away.

"She's good."

"Job okay?"

There it was. That knowing. It wasn't odd to assume we'd talk about work, but there was something in the tone. As if asking were a politeness and she already had the details.

Her hand stroked over my back as I reached for the faucet, intending to wash some dishes. I shuddered, leaning back into her. The world started to slide fuzzy. All these concerns made no sense. All of these questions and insecurities were useless. This was my Tia, and she loved me.

A sound lit up the house, like a giant but muffled pop. Tianna spun, her hand still resting on my back. I turned carefully, tangling my fingers in hers.

Four beautiful men stood in the kitchen. Knee length black hair, cheekbones that could cut, and eyes just as damned mercurial as Tia's. They wore matching uniforms in stark black with leaf green trim. And each one of them had delicately pointed ears. They ignored me, keeping their disapproving collective gaze on my partner.

"Tianna of the Southern Shores, you are bid return to complete your sentence as the queen's Distraction."

Their voices slid over my senses, oily and difficult to grasp. I struggled to follow their words.

Tia's were all too clear as she laughed, loud and bright. "A decade of letting that creature use me as her plaything? I think not. I am perfectly content here. She has scarred me enough."

The four shifted into formation and took one step forward. Tia held up a hand.

"Will the queen entertain an alternative?"

I should have been listening more, paying more attention. But the whole scene was so surreal and foreign, I barely held on to reality. I missed her intent.

One of the royal guards lowered his lids and tilted his head back. When he opened his eyes, they had changed to a golden amber. The voice that poured from his lips was glorious and feminine.

"I will. What have you in mind, scratch?"

Alarms began screaming in my head. The room felt smaller and much, much warmer. I stumbled as Tianna tugged me forward but kept my feet under me. The golden-eyed guard looked me over carefully. Finally, he blinked, and his eyes returned to his own.

"She accepts. The human will serve out your turn."

Hands wrapped around my arms, cold and unyielding.

Tianna pulled her fingers from mine. "Keep her, then and label my debt fully paid. I have no use for her any longer."

My kitchen, my garden, my home all faded away. I desperately wished my love for her would remain behind with them, but for the rest of my days, the ache for her would weigh more heavily than any cruelty the fae queen crafted.

FINDING HER
By Matt Lucas

A blue globe adorned with wisps of white and masses of green and brown hung against a captivating black backdrop. Glistening stars ornamented the immense void. Among them were two sentient orbs crafted of spirit's brilliant light.

"I'm going to miss you when I'm

down there," the spirit of a woman soon to be born lamented.

"I'll be with you there soon enough," her male counterpart assured.

"You know what happens when we go to Earth," she mourned. "We won't remember each other."

"We'll find each other," he comforted despite the uncertainty that clouded his soul.

"How?" she probed. "I'm going to the south of the southwest continent and you're assigned to the northern region of the northwest. Now that distance looks like nothing, but down there it seems insurmountable."

"Have faith," he answered with hope.

In the sudden twinkling of the stars, she glimmered brighter. A dazzling array of coloured chords of light surrounded her spirit. Awe struck as her supernova swelled before launching her towards Earth like a fiery comet.

A bittersweet concoction of joy and grief bubbled within his spirit. Turning towards the cosmos, he cried out in prayer to God. "Bring her back to me someday. Give me a sign...anything so I know her when I find her."

"D-D-D-D-D-D!" A sudden, blaring horn resonated through the ether.

Matt lurched forward with wide eyes and panting breaths. Wiping the sweat from his brow, the man cursed himself for continuing to use the obnoxious alarm. Grasping his phone, Matt shut off the alarm as the memory of the recurring dream cycled through his mind. There was a name that lingered on the tip of his tongue. It felt like knowing the answer to a test question, but not being able to recall it in full until you heard it aloud.

Brushing off the vision, Matt laid back into bed and examined his phone. His hopeful heart fluttered at the prospect of a message from someone, anyone who might cure his loneliness. When he found nothing, his heart's wings floundered and plummeted to the pit of his stomach.

A disheartened sigh billowed from his nostrils as he rolled from bed to start his day. On his drive to work, Matt couldn't shake the bizarre dream that purveyed his sleep from time to time. It was like a memory from a forgotten time and place.

Once at his desk, Matt sat with an open journal to jot down his prayers before the clamour of employees and ringing phones erupted through the office. Hopeful eyes bounced between the empty page and his phone. Still, there were no messages. He hung his head as his heart sunk. A desperate yearning for the companionship that eluded him for 27 years left a strained tightness in his chest.

That's when a light tapping jostled Matt from the desperate thoughts that barraged his mind. Whirling around, he saw his bespectacled colleague, Josh. "Sorry to bother you," Josh interrupted as he scratched at the sandy stubble on his chin, "I just wanted to introduce you to our new hire, Daniela."

Stepping out from behind Josh was an olive-skinned, brown-eyed beauty. Straight, chestnut hair framed her kind, round face adorned with striking eyebrows and rosy cheeks. She wore a simple black blouse paired with grey slacks.

"Daniela," Matt breathed as if the name had lingered on his tongue, unspoken for a lifetime.

"It's nice to meet you," Daniela introduced herself in an accent Matt wasn't familiar with.

She leaned in and extended her hand towards him. As their hands clasped, Daniela's necklace leapt into the open. Multi-coloured chords of light gleamed off the golden cross ornamented by a circle of glimmering gems.

"Nice to meet you too," Matt replied with a smile. "Where are you from?"

Daniela's head bobbed back and forth. "I was born in Argentina but moved to

Florida as a teenager. What about you?"

"Pittsburgh," Matt answered. "I moved here a couple years ago."

Daniela smiled, making a flock of butterflies soar in his stomach. "So, you went south, and I came north," she observed.

Matt chuckled. "Glad we could meet in the middle."

"It was nice to meet you." Daniela couldn't wipe the look of happiness from her face. "I hope I see you around."

Matt nodded, returning Daniela's infectious grin. "You will."

When she left, Matt turned back to his journal. Exhilarated nerves made his hands quake. As he wrote down Daniela's name, he couldn't shake the joyous feeling of a prayer answered.

Over the coming weeks, friendship blossomed. In the streaking of a fiery comet, it morphed into affection. Soon, the companion Matt sought wasn't just within his grasp, she was standing in his arms beneath a clear night's sky.

"What do you think it'll be like when we get up there?" Daniela asked. "Do you think we'll remember each other?"

"We found each other down here," Matt replied with certainty as he pulled her in close. "It won't be any different up there."

"It might look so small from here," Daniela pondered, "but up there the distance is insurmountable."

"Have faith," Matt assured as he planted his lips onto hers.

When their embrace ceased, Daniela

rested her head on Matt's chest. "I do."

Loving warmth permeated both of their hearts. They were entangled beneath the stars like a divine knot that no man could untie. Together, they were whole.

Matt raised his eyes to the cosmos. His spirit leapt with joy and sent a grateful prayer to God, who'd brought them together by fate.

Thank you.

57 MINUTES
By N.M. Brown

For as long as I can remember, the only newspaper I've ever been excited about is the Sunday paper. It has everything—coupons, births, deaths (that one's not so fun), comics, etc. The Record has a delivery option where you only pay for and receive the paper on Sundays. So, naturally

I took advantage.

The coupons this week are kinda shitty to be honest. My husband, Charles, and I always spent Sundays together. Each week it started the same way. He was on his phone looking at most likely the very same news that I held in the paper I read. He wasn't old school like I was.

I love being able to actually hold things in my hands—books, newspapers, DVDs and the like. Everything's online these days. It terrifies me to think that most likely when our two girls are grown, books won't be common anymore, a relic of the past like the Atari or the Video Cassette. It's even more unsettling to know that most likely, people won't even care.

This particular Sunday starts like any other. I've just bought myself a red dress with yellow sunflowers and am taking the opportunity to show it off to Charles. He donned his black Dickie pants that seem to withstand the tests of time. He's had them since before I've known him. I've given up on straightening my hair after almost burning it off last month, it's tight curls hang over my shoulders.

I have a paper routine that I follow methodically. First, I go to the coupons, then the comics, then the birth announcements, then the deaths to make sure there's no one I know, and I save the articles for last.

The comics are okay this week. Garfield is still being a grump and Dilbert's still being Dilbert. Dave Grandlund depicts a cartoon Smokey the Bear lying on his back with a bullet hole in his chest. A family of tourists is shown behind him, the father holding a smoking gun in the air. The quote bubble reads: "Oops! From a distance, he looked threatening." Okay… Little political for a comics section, aren't we? They can't all be winners, I guess. A sigh escapes my lips as I hand that section to Charles.

"Sheesh," he mutters. "Kinda rough on Smokey this week, weren't they?"

Only one birth this week, a baby boy named William! There's no picture… Bummer. I always love it when the birth announcements are boys. Every birth is a beautiful miracle, but we don't have a boy of our own, so it's nice to read about.

"Only one birth this week," I tell my husband absent mindedly.

"Oh?" His eyebrows raise in surprise.

"Is it a boy? I swear the last month's been nothing but girls."

"It is!" I reply.

His eyes twinkle from the wide smile I'm so deeply in love with.

There are three deaths in the obituary section. One stands alone. The other two are posted separately but linked together; a caption underneath says CONTINUED ON 4A. I've never seen that before. Well, I was on my way to the articles anyway, so… I feed into my morbid curiosity.

4A—An elderly sleeping couple is pictured in two separate hospital beds. The beds are close enough together that the couple can hold hands. The headline reads: ELDERLY COUPLE PASSES AWAY 57 MINUTES APART HOLDING HANDS ON THEIR DEATHBEDS.

"Awww, Charlie, this is so sad but sweet at the same time. Here…look." I toss him the paper, already folded open to 4A. His reading face softens as he finishes reading the article. "Damn Maggie… That is sad. I hope that's how we go when it's our time." He smiles at me. "I'm sorry babe but that's not gonna happen; you're practically an old man as it is." I blow him a kiss and wink.

Charles's face drops. "Maggie, did you look at this picture?"

I nod, "Yeah… What about it?"

His eyes widen with over-exaggerated disbelief.

"Look at the blanket. We have the same one! Creepy, huh?"

I take the paper out of his hands to look for myself.

Sure enough, a large yellow blanket with grey circles lay over both their beds. I look over to our couch for confirmation even though none is needed. It's the same one. My eyes begin to focus on other details in the picture. The elderly man wore a white button up short-sleeved shirt. His black pants are visible from the bottom of the blanket.

My eyes drift to the woman now. My heart feels like it literally drops to my stomach but freezes just before it hits the bottom. The elderly woman was wearing a very worn, faded from what once must have been a vibrant red dress...with yellow sunflowers. Two hellishly creepy coincidences for sure, but not impossible… A bad omen at the very most. I revert my gaze to the small, printed text of the article.

Tears stab my eyes like needles and a scream bellows through my lungs. The names of the elderly couple…are Charles and Margaret Welsh.

Fishtails

By Stacey Jaine McIntosh

The full moon shimmered silvery bright, casting a long shadow over the ocean. This was Poseidon's domain. This watery abode, so full of fish and merfolk, while lovely to behold it would never be home to Aphrodite. As hard as she tried and as much as she loved him, she would always prefer the feel of sand between her toes to that of the saltwater brine as it filled her nostrils. Swimming, although it came easy to her, was not how she wished to spend her days. And with one last look she said goodbye to her love forever.

CHANGELING
By V.A. Vazquez

Brody stared out the window at the woods that sprung up behind the parking lot. His banged-up Dodge Caravan was parked at the border where asphalt gave way to stringy blades of grass. A few steps forward would lead you past the saplings, tall and thin like wooden yardsticks planted in the dirt, and then a few more would bring you into the forest proper: the mighty wych elms with their gnarled trunks, puckered with knot-like tumours. There were rumours that faeries lived in those woods, beyond the wych elms and across the stream that bubbled all the way to the church graveyard.

As the bell rang, he shoved his books deep into his backpack and headed out the classroom door. He'd packed a water bottle and some home-baked shortbread cakes, as well as a GPS in case he got lost. He shouldn't get lost; the idea he even *could* get lost was absurd. But he packed it anyway just in case. He pushed through the front doors of the school and into the summer afternoon. The parking lot smelled of diesel fuel and dust as engines roared to life and students peeled out from between the yellow lines.

"Hey, Brody!" He turned to see one of the guys from the AV club standing next to his pickup truck. He'd piled camera equipment into the back and was securing a tarp over it. "We're headed to the beach to get some B-roll. Wanna come along?"

"No thanks," he shouted back. "I have to finish up some chores around the house."

"We could grab some booze on the way. Celebrate your birthday?"

"Maybe next time."

His friend gave him a quick nod before hopping into the front seat of the truck and speeding away. Soon the parking lot had emptied out with the exception of teachers who hung around to grade papers or plan their lessons. Brody double-checked his car to make sure the doors were locked up tight, and then he stepped into the woods.

Back when he'd been little, when the memories were still fresh, this had felt natural: the soft sponge of moss underneath his sneakers, the birds chirping overhead in the tree branches, the scent of algae whipping up from the stream. But it had been so long now. He stumbled over toppled logs when before, he would have leapt over them with no trouble.

Fuck him, Brody thought, tugging his sneaker free from the mud.

He walked through the woods until he came to the stream. This was usually where folks from the village would turn back, retreat to the safety and familiarity of their homes; to venture beyond the stream was to invite all sorts of trouble. However, trouble was exactly what Brody was looking for. He hitched his backpack higher and began to pick his way over the stones that littered the bed of the stream. They were slick, and the rubber soles of his sneakers didn't have a particularly good grip. It only took a few steps before his feet slipped out from under him, and he tumbled into the water.

"*Shit!*" he yelled and then slapped his hand over his mouth. He scanned the treeline to make sure no one had heard him. Nothing. No cracks of fallen branches, no quivering of leaves. He double-checked his backpack to make sure the shortbread cakes hadn't got wet and continued across the stream.

He knew the spot when he arrived. The

path through the woods may have been fuzzy, buried deep in his memory, but he could never forget this glen. Moss-covered boulders broke through the ground on both sides, towering above him, while the stream babbled a few meters away. Sunlight dappled the forest floor, but there was no birdsong. No chitter-chatter of little animals. Not here.

Brody shrugged off his backpack and unzipped the top. Taking out the shortbread cakes, he laid one in the centre of the glen and tucked himself behind a nearby wych elm. Then he waited—so still, you wouldn't have believed it possible for a teenager.

That's when he saw him.

The boy crept out of the bushes. His feet pounded on the moss, and his fingers snapped branches as he pushed them aside. Even after all these years, he stumbled through the woods like livestock. His head was covered in a mess of shaggy black curls, little twigs poking through the tangles. Brody readied himself behind the wych elm.

The boy shifted forward, his stare never leaving the shortbread cake. He reached out, and right as his fingers wrapped around the crumbly crust, Brody leapt onto him. He wasn't quick enough to get away; no amount of time spent living in the woods could stamp out the weakness of humanity. "I've fucking got you," Brody hissed, as he wrapped an arm around the boy's neck, wrestling him to the ground. "Give up already."

The boy writhed like an eel in his grip,

his naked flesh covered in slippery muck. But Brody just dug his knees in further and braced himself. Finally, the boy managed to contort his spine enough to look into his captor's eyes.

Brody had thought he was prepared for this moment.

He wasn't.

The eyes that looked up into his were his own. Not *quite* his own, even faerie magic couldn't stretch that far, but close enough to make Brody shudder. They had the same black curly hair, although Brody's had been tamed with pomade. The same caterpillar-thick eyebrows. Brody's cheeks were more hollowed-out than his doppelgänger's, his limbs slightly longer and stringier, but they were similar enough that Brody's grip went a little slack.

The boy took his chance.

He pushed back against Brody, shoving him down into the dirt as he struggled to get free. Brody rutted his fingernails into the boy's shoulder. "Stop!" the boy shouted, twisting this way and that. "You're hurting me!"

"I don't care."

Finally, the boy collapsed in a heap against Brody's chest. The two of them laid there for a few minutes, their heavy panting the only sound that could be heard in the faerie glen. "Fine," the boy said. "You've got me."

That was enough. Brody released his hold, and the boy, *Broderick*, scrambled a safe distance away. He couldn't go too far though; that would be breaking the rules. And faerie or not, he wouldn't be allowed to return if he broke the rules. They both crouched on the ground, sizing each other up. Trying to pick out the small differences that distinguished one from the other.

"You're him," Broderick said at last.

"Yes."

"Why did you come back here?"

"Why do you think?"

Broderick's nose scrunched up into a grimace. Brody wondered if that's how he looked when his mother, *Broderick's* mother, told him to take out the garbage or finish his homework.

"I'm not leaving."

"Oh yes, you are—"

"No, I'm not. They made their choice seventeen years ago. They chose *me* and left you behind."

Brody scrubbed a hand through his

hair, the grime on his fingertips smearing off along his scalp. "You don't know *shit.*"

"I know faeries don't swear."

"Oh, fuck off, you sanctimonious little prick. You try living seventeen years on the outside and see if you're still knitting flower crowns."

"I wouldn't know."

"No, you wouldn't. Because you came barging in here with your cute chubby baby-cheeks and stole my home." Brody pushed himself up to his feet, his sneakers sinking unsteadily into the moss. "Your mother knew. Ever since the day they switched us out. I was too colicky, too scrawny, to be her little Broderick."

"Well, they didn't send you back, so—"

"Of course they didn't send me back! It's the twenty-first century. You think the police are going to look the other way while a family abandons their infant in the woods? No one believes in fucking faeries anymore. Your mother would have been locked up in a psychiatric ward, and I would have been put in foster care."

Broderick snuffled a little and shifted back even further into the bushes, getting ready to sprint away as soon as he could. "I never asked to leave," he said, as if that made it any better.

"Sure you did. You asked every time you reached your greedy little hands up to grab at their wings. Every time you got pixie-dust lodged underneath those fingernails of yours."

"Did yours ever come in?"

Brody bit down hard on the inside of his cheek and shook his head.

"Mine neither."

"Of course yours never came in, you idiot. You're human. Just because you live with us doesn't make you one of us."

Broderick looked like he was going to argue but shrugged one shoulder instead. Brody was never able to figure out why his wings hadn't come in when he'd reached adolescence. Maybe he'd been on the outside for too long; maybe distance had changed him into something else.

No, he thought. *You know who you are, what you are. Nothing can take that away from you.*

"So, what do you want?" Broderick asked. And then before Brody could say anything: "I'm not leaving. And you can't make me."

"All I'd have to do is bind you, and

you'd be stuck here. Just like I've been all these years."

"You wouldn't."

"Fuck you. Of course I would."

Broderick seemed to realise he was trapped then, like an animal that'd got its ankle snapped in a snare.

"I don't want to go back."

"Why not? You don't even know what it's like on the outside."

"I know everything I need to."

"Don't you miss your mother?"

Brody thought about the woman who'd bought him crayons and colouring books, all the trappings of a normal childhood. She'd volunteered with his Boy Scout troop and joined the middle school PTA. But something had always felt *wrong* in their household. Postpartum depression, the psychiatrists had said, but that hadn't been it. He'd overheard her talking to another mother on the playground once, complaining that she couldn't connect with her child the way she was supposed to. *Don't worry,* the other mother had said, resting a dishwater-rough hand over hers. *It'll come in time.*

It never had.

"I don't even remember my mother," Broderick said. "What's she like?"

Distant.

"She used to spend hours at the window, trying to catch a glimpse of you. She always told me she just liked the woods, but I knew what she was looking for out there."

"Oh." Broderick slumped down onto the forest floor. "So, you want to come back? Is that it?"

"I don't *want* to come back. I *am* coming back. That's why I'm here."

"I don't think they're going to let you in."

"Of course they will. I'm one of them."

But a wych elm knot started twisting deep in Brody's stomach, its lumpy wood and sharp little twigs pressing into his guts. They had to let him back in, right? Once he came of age? He'd been counting down the days for the past seventeen years.

"You can try."

Brody walked up to the birch tree that stood in the centre of the glen. To any casual observer, it was just another tree: cream-coloured bark speckled with black patches, leaves casting a greenish tint over the forest floor. But Brody knew better. He reached his palm out but stopped just short of pressing against the wood.

"What are you waiting for?" Broderick asked.

"Nothing. Just give me a second."

"You haven't forgotten how to go through, have you? You just press your palm—"

"I haven't forgotten! For fuck's sake, just give me a second!"

Brody stared hard at the birch tree. He'd spent so many years waiting for the moment when he'd press his palm against the bark and return home. But now that he was standing here . . .

"Fuck it," he said and pressed his palm up against the birch, right on the gnarled knot of wood where he remembered the doorway being.

Nothing happened.

Again, he pushed against the wood, waiting for the bark to split and the entrance to be revealed. Nothing. He turned to Broderick: "This is the right tree?"

Broderick nodded.

Maybe it's just stuck, he thought, bracing his feet in the muck and putting the entire weight of his body behind the shove. But even as his sneakers slid backwards, he knew. The door wasn't stuck; they weren't going to let him back in. He balled up his fist and punched the bark. Once, twice, three times. His knuckles caught on the rough patches, and the skin shredded until the knobbiest bits were burning and smeared with blood. *"Let me in!"* he shouted, going at the birch like it was a speed-bag at the gym. *"You fucking dicks! Let me back in!"*

But if they heard him, calling from the outside, no one responded.

"Told you they wouldn't."

He turned towards Broderick who was still crouched on the ground, picking off bits of the shortcake and shoving them into his mouth. His greedy little mouth that'd been stuffed full of cow's milk and honeycomb, while he'd been given Enfamil formula from a bottle. "You son of a bitch—"

Before Broderick had time to react, Brody tackled him to the ground, yanking the shortbread out of his hand and throwing it deep into the woods. He curled his hand up into a fist and knocked it straight into Broderick's jaw. Broderick let out a surprised little *"oomph"*, which made Brody wonder if he'd ever felt pain before.

He punched him again.

"You stole my home—" *Punch.* "My family—" *Punch.* "My entire fucking life—"

Broderick had managed to get one hand free and was blocking his face, absorbing the worst of the blows. "Get off me!" he yelled. "*Help!*"

"They can't hear you." Brody pinned Broderick's wrist to the ground, forcing it down into the mud. "Even if they could, they wouldn't give a damn."

"Yes, they would. I'm—"

"*You're not one of us!*"

"*Neither are you!*"

The two of them stared at each other. They both had eyes the colour of birch leaves at the height of summer, when the sunshine caught on their ragged edges. Brody hadn't been born with these eyes; he couldn't remember what colour his had been before being exiled to the outside. He had been given Broderick's face, abandoned in his crib one night, left to cry for his parents until toddlerhood when he realised crying would do no good. No one was coming back for him.

And now, he couldn't return to them either.

Broderick wasn't actually a faerie, no matter how much he wanted to be, but the strictures that governed his people still applied to him.

"Your true name is Broderick Liam Abernathy," he said, and Broderick's eyes went as wide as skipping stones.

"No," he said. "*No, no, no, no!*"

"And I hereby bind—"

"Stop!"

"You to my—"

Brody didn't have the chance to complete the binding incantation, the one humans sometimes used to capture faerie servants or concubines. Instead, Broderick jammed his heel into the mud and used the leverage to push himself up. So that his lips were pressed firmly against Brody's.

Brody let out a muffled yelp of indignation, but Broderick's ploy worked. His grip slackened; the words dried up in his mouth like the riverbed in summer's high heat. Broderick could have made his escape, but he seemed just as surprised as Brody. Their eyes remained open, green meeting green, as they both decided what should happen next.

Brody shoved his doppelgänger down deeper into the moss and pressed his tongue into the crease of his closed lips. Broderick opened his mouth, letting Brody taste the memory of shortbread on his tongue. *Typical,* Brody thought, ripping away the clothes that had been stitched together from leaves and flower petals. Faeries were lustful by nature, and while Broderick wasn't actually a faerie, he was bound to imitate what he'd seen. He slipped his thigh in-between Broderick's, letting him grind up against the fabric of his jeans.

"Do you like that?" he asked, rutting his own hardness into the crevice of Broderick's hip. "Filthy fucking faerie." Broderick reached up and looped his hands around the back of Brody's neck, closing his eyes and rolling his hips against his captor.

It should have been stranger—fucking a copy of himself so perfect no one but his own mother had been able to tell the difference. But there *were* differences. While Broderick was healthy and pink-cheeked, the way a human should be, Brody's skin was the same colour as the lunulae on fingernails, the whitish crescent-moons leading to the roots. He'd always looked sickly, even when he'd been well-fed and well-fucked.

"I'm not letting you go," Brody whispered into the flesh of Broderick's throat. "You're mine now. I'll drag you back to the parking lot, kicking and screaming, and toss you into my trunk. When we get back home, I'll lock you in the basement and have my way with you every day."

Broderick moaned again. But Brody wasn't sure what was driving him wild: the idea of repeating this encounter . . .

Or the idea of returning to the outside. Of being forced, against his will, to return to the outside. Maybe Broderick was just as homesick as he'd been, but he couldn't admit it to anyone, not even himself. But if Brody *forced* him, wrapped his fist through those black curls and pulled him across the forest floor like a brute, then he'd never have to admit it to anyone.

Broderick shuddered, and Brody felt dampness splatter onto denim. He followed soon after against his zipper, wetness spreading out across his crotch.

He could still do it. Bind Broderick

and make sure he couldn't travel through the birch, not without his permission. But then what would he do with him? *That's* his *problem*, Broderick thought. *He can hitch a ride to the city and beg on the street corner like everyone else who doesn't have a home.*

But the thought left Brody feeling empty.

He couldn't travel through the birch. He was stuck on the outside. Trapping Broderick here wouldn't solve his problem.

"Go on," he said, wiping his nose with his bloodied and muck-covered knuckles. "Get."

Broderick hesitated for a moment, and Brody wondered if he was going to volunteer to stay back of his own accord. But then he scrambled over towards the birch, still crouched on all fours, and readied his hand to press against the same patch of bark that'd denied an actual faerie only moments before.

But he didn't touch the birch.

Instead, he turned back to look at Brody.

"You should come here again," he said, his voice low as if they might be overheard. "Next week maybe."

"What?"

"Come back. I'll be waiting."

And then, without giving Brody time to respond, he pressed his palm against the birch and disappeared through an entrance Brody could no longer see.

Brody pushed himself up off the ground, trying his best to brush the filth from his clothes. With one last look at the birch tree, he took the remaining shortbread cakes out of his backpack and left them in the glen. He'd bring more next week when he returned. Then, he hoisted his backpack up onto his shoulders and started back down the path towards his Dodge Caravan and the house that'd never been his home.

BAD MOON RISING
By Vonnie Winslow Crist

Darlene glanced at the clock hanging over the register. It was after eleven, and the last customer was still perched on a stool at the luncheon counter eating pie. She finished sopping up the coffee, cider, and cola puddles from the tabletop of the booth nearest the door and pulled down the window shades hiding from view the jack-o'-lantern, black cat, and owl cut-outs stuck on the storefront glass. Then she walked in back of the counter and slid her pencil and order pad onto the top shelf beside the bins containing sugar and artificial sweetener packets.

"Thanks," said the elderly customer from behind her. "That was real good."

"You're welcome, Mr Suddi. See you tomorrow night."

"Right, tomorrow," the old man replied as he stood, buttoned up his sweater, then shuffled out the front door of *Raleigh's Delight*.

Darlene took off her apron, hung it on a peg, then leaned over to check her make-up in the chrome of the carbonated beverage dispenser. She liked to look at herself in the chrome—the faint crows-feet around her eyes were not visible. The mirrors in the ladies' room made her look thirty. But why shouldn't they? She was thirty-six.

Pushing open the swinging door to the kitchen, she hollered, "Everybody is out. I'm leaving."

She spotted the diner's owner, Stan Raleigh, scrubbing the griddle. Darlene liked that he did not just hire street kids to do all the dirty work, instead he pitched in and did some of the messy chores, too.

Stan looked up from the greasy slab of steel and asked, "Register closed down?"

"Yeah. Closed it before Mr Suddamendala left. Tape is in the drawer."

"Tape," she muttered to herself. If the

freaking grid had not gone down and screwed things up, computers would still be doing all the work.

"Thanks. Have a good night," called Stan from the sink as he suds up a scrub brush. "Don't forget to lock the door on the way out, especially tonight."

"No problem. But there shouldn't be any trouble, by now the trick-or-treaters are sleeping in their pods," Darlene responded as she reached under the luncheon counter and grabbed her pocketbook.

Darlene strolled out of *Raleigh's Delight* and slammed the front door. Slamming was not optional—since the door never locked if you closed it gentle-like. She jiggled the handle, just to double-check, and then nodded at the cardboard skeleton jitterbugging on the other side of the door's glass pane. Finally off duty, she tugged the rubber band out of her hair. She wore her hair tied back when waitressing, but when not at work, she loved the silky way it felt against her neck.

Darlene hurried down the sidewalk, smiling at the full moon that hung like a dinner plate on the wall of night. The 11:20 shuttle should be by any minute, and she was eager to get home. After popping a piece of gum in her mouth, she looked at her watch: *11:21 pm.*

Tonight, she needed to be home on time—she was expecting company. Plus, she had forgotten to refill her ferret's bowl of dried kibbles. Not that the ferret was thin. Darlene suspected she had one of the few fat ferrets on the planet. Still, she worried that Claude might get into more trouble than usual if she was late.

When she heard the squeal of brakes as the shuttle operator began to slow the mass-trans vehicle, she spit out her gum, wrapped it in a tissue, tossed it into a nearby waste bin, unwrapped a second piece, put the new gum in her mouth, and slid its wrapper into her uniform's pocket. Two pieces of gum would normally be excessive, but fresh breath was important tonight.

The shuttle pulled up to the curb, and Darlene got on and slipped into a seat about midway back. She crossed her legs, then pushed her uniform's skirt down towards her knees. It was not that she was modest, she just figured most people didn't want to see white-stockinged legs. For some reason, Stan thought white shoes and hose complimented the white cotton aprons his waitresses wore over their turquoise retro-look uniforms. And so, Darlene and the other waitresses at *Raleigh's Delight* wore the ugly things.

The shuttle had gone six blocks, when the driver stomped on the brakes to avoid smashing into a scooter which had suddenly changed lanes. Darlene grabbed the seat in front of her as the vehicle lurched. Across the aisle, a boy in his early twenties yelled a profanity. When he slipped a headset off his ears, she heard drums, guitars, and singing. With the volume turned up so loud, she suspected he would go deaf and have an artificial eardrum installed within a few years. Without warning, the music boy looked at Darlene and caught her staring.

She pressed her back against the seat and turned her face to the window. Outside, the darkened glass, neon signs glowed red-orange, green, and purple as the shuttle zipped down the boulevard. Darlene knew if she had been walking by those storefronts instead of speeding along in a mass-trans vehicle, she would have heard the hum of the tubing. She supposed the hum had to do with the gas the manufacturers sealed in the glass tubes, but she wasn't sure of the science.

She knew the tubing was heated and formed. If you looked closely, you could see the glass near the connectors was singed and blackened. But few people noticed the dark glass—most only saw the colourful designs.

Shifting in her seat, she turned her

attention to the reflections on the inside of the shuttle's tinted windows. She studied the images of the passengers, noting there were about twenty people on the shuttle, including some in costume. Two seats back, a young couple was kissing.

Her mouth curled as she remembered evenings spent with Jimmy Tyler beneath the trees in Uncle Cally's agro-orchard where the fruit hung dark and sweet. Jimmy, ha! She licked her lips. For a moment, she thought she felt him pressed up against her arm and touched the plastic seat next to her thigh to make sure he hadn't got onto the vehicle without her noticing.

Darlene squinted, then looked at the window reflections again. The music boy was moving his head to the thumping beat coming from his earphones. Jimmy had done the same thing to songs by old-time rockers like Creedence Clearwater Revival. Last time she saw him, about an hour before he left for the hunting trip with his cousins, he was singing Bad *Moon Rising.* She had told him to wear red, but he was never one for caution.

If only Jimmy had listened, she thought. *Then things might have gone differently.*

The shuttle lurched again. A quick glance at the street markers told her the next stop was hers. She looked across the aisle. The music boy was still there, and he was studying her. Ignoring his stares, she stood and moved to the front of the shuttle. The vehicle hissed to a stop; she got off, then began to walk down Church Street.

It was about two blocks to her living quarters in an old warehouse which had been converted into six apartments. Usually, it was a pleasant stroll by three churches, a few Victorian-styled homes, and the Veterans Memorial Park. The VM Park occupied an odd-shaped grassy lot that had a few trees and shrubs, a fountain, some benches, and a memorial statue with the names of local war heroes engraved on bronze plaques attached to its base. Darlene liked to sit on one of its benches on her days off and read the paperback novels she picked up from Like New Second-Hand Books.

But tonight, the park's peacefulness was suddenly disrupted by raucous voices coming from behind her. Darlene stopped, then turned around. The music boy and two other men were following her.

"Hey," the music boy called. "Where're you going in such a hurry?"

"Didn't you hear what my friend said?" asked one of the others.

Darlene bit her lip and walked as fast as she could. She saw the door to her apartment was only about fifty meters away.

"Slow down. We just want to ask you a question," said the music boy. He was about two meters behind her now.

Darlene looked for Jimmy but saw no one on the street. She knew it wouldn't do any good to scream, so she broke into a run. The trio following her gave a whoop, and then began to run, too. She had started up the steps to her door when one of the young men grabbed her shoulder.

Darlene reached into her purse, grasped the cold handle of one of Jimmy Tyler's old guns. She turned around to face her assailants. Security cameras had fallen victim to techno glitches associated with the grid failure. Thieves had made off with any remaining usable parts months ago, so whatever happened next, would remain a mystery.

The music boy grinned at her. Darlene noticed the gleam from her porch lantern was reflected by the blade of a knife he held in his left hand. Thankful that Jimmy had taught her how to shoot, Darlene pursed her lips and pulled the trigger.

The music boy fell like an apple to the ground. His two friends vanished, just like the mourners had after Jimmy's funeral. And Darlene was alone. She looked down at the body sprawled on the steps. The boy was obviously dead—dead and staring up at the stars.

As Darlene slid Jimmy's revolver back into her pocketbook, she recalled how Jimmy and she used to stare at the stars on August nights when the lawns were speckled with fireflies and owls, tree frogs, and cicada filled the air with song. She smiled. Those had been the best days of her life.

She heard a cough, or maybe it was the scuff of a shoe, and peered towards the corner of Church and Cemetery Streets. There was Jimmy, still young and handsome, standing beneath the streetlight in the plaid shirt she had given him for his eighteenth birthday. He raised his hand. Darlene sighed and returned his greeting.

A siren in the distance caused her pulse to race as she stared down Church Street towards the main road. The emergency vehicle's whining reminded her of the siren on the ambulance that had taken Jimmy to the medical centre the day he was shot—the day he had first left. As the shrill noise became fainter, her heart returned to its normal slow thumping, and she looked back at the corner. Jimmy was striding towards her.

Darlene wiped away the tears that threatened to spill down her cheeks. Tonight, the night when the dead could pass through the veil that separated them from the living, Jimmy would visit with Claude and her from the stroke of midnight until first light. Then, she'd accompany him back to the graveyard, kiss him one final time, and spend the next three-hundred-and-sixty-four days waiting for October thirty-first to roll around again.

Jimmy was strolling up the sidewalk to her door, and just before she felt his strong arms wrap around her, Darlene bent down, closed the music boy's eyes. Before going inside, Jimmy and she would carry the body to the graveyard and leave it leaning against a tombstone. It was an easy task, for she'd chosen the location of her apartment with care—just across the street from the town's oldest cemetery.

Darlene hoped the dead boy had someone who loved him, someone to visit next Halloween. She shivered as Jimmy's lips met hers. But before she lowered her eyelids, Darlene glanced over his shoulder. In the glow of the Harvest Moon, she saw the music boy. His ghost had risen. It gaped at her with a confused look in its dark glassy eyes, and then, it turned and wandered down the trash-littered street.

First published, *Owl Light*, Cold Moon Press, 2014

I WILL LOVE YOU
By Ximena Escobar

I closed my eyes to the redness, listened to the fire that I lost all sense of my surroundings but that of the warm memory of our closeness.

I heard his steps approaching, saw the orange reflections stretch on his glass as the red wine swirled and we toasted to the future—his eyes, sparkling like yours used to sparkle.

I smiled, disguising my longing for you. Is it really you, breathing in my ear? Yesterday marked the beginning of a new love, but the flames, darling, will always be ours.

As long as fire burns, I will love you.

AGNES'S SONG
By A.L. O'Connor

"Did you write anything today?" asked Agnes, the beautiful Highland lass who was his lover and had crossed five hundred years to see him.

"I did! The first part of my climax chapter. I'm finally getting the writer's juice flowing thanks to you, my writing muse," the widower Garrett Jensen happily said. He vibrated with excitement and reached out to crush her in a big embrace. He picked her up and dumped her on the bed, eagerly divesting her of the medieval raiment, the ties and corset no longer foreign.

Garrett had taken this remote cabin in the Scottish Highlands. It was a modest affair, just one room with the kitchen being just a small sink and one bank of shelves. There was a damaged kitchen table set under the only window in the room. A worn bed with a shabby quilt stood in the corner. Unknown to Garrett, the cottage was a gateway to medieval Scotland due to the Druids' stones located within walking distance. A fact that Agnes knew and took advantage of because she was a Druid.

Agnes kissed Garrett back with recklessness, thankful that in this time the men were better lovers than the inexperienced and overly anxious ones in her time. Garrett for his part loved that Agnes was uncomplicated, not like the women from his time. Each felt fulfilled. They took off each other's clothes and fell onto the bed where it groaned under their weight. They made love fast and finished laughing, sated, and happy.

"You are sure this won't get you in trouble with your family? Because your visits and our romantic dalliance is helping me to get over writer's block." Garrett breathed into Agnes's neck.

Agnes smirked. "No, we do this and

then get married. Only the priests are spared knowing. If a 'maid' gets pregnant, we hurry to the actual wedding. It all works out."

"How did you find out about this cottage?" Garrett looked at her curiously.

"My Gran is a wise woman and a Druid. She has the lore from the Druids, and she knows the secret of corners that solidify and manipulate magic. The standing stones, the blue Saracens, next to this cottage is such a corner. She has taught me the lore, so I am also a Druid," explained Agnes.

"Whoever you are, your magic has kept my imagination going substantially. For that, I am grateful and happy! I give you a heartfelt thank you. Now I can get my manuscript to my editor and get them happily off my back." Garrett rolled over and uncomfortably laid on the too narrow, too short bed.

Outside the view was stunning, rolling hills blanketed in heather and thistle. In the distance, dark mountains were rising to shoulder their rocks against the icy winds from the north. Sitting in a dank mountain lair, the dragon stirred awake, stood up to his two-story height, and stretched out his wings giving them a flap. After doing that, the dragon thought about his internment. He thought about the Druids and how they were able to cast a spell to put him to sleep for five hundred years; then he sent out his magic to see what was going on and who broke his sleeping spell. He found Agnes and her writer lover. "What could be better than to make the writer's inspiration leave? I think I shall exert my magic and cause him to have writer's block." The scaly, dark-winged dragon performed arcane rituals, the spell was concocted, and the dragon sent it out on a spume of flame.

***

The next day Agnes bounded into Garrett's cottage with dire news. "My magic notified me that the dragon who has been sleeping for five hundred years has just woken from his long slumber. I helped the Druids cast the spell to put him in his rest. It could be now that I have used that same magic to cross time and meet you, and it had dire consequences on that dragon's spell. He is awake. Have you felt anything amiss?"

"I tried to write this morning, but I find I'm having writer's block. This shouldn't be happening because I know how the chapter should be resolved, but I couldn't write!" Garrett spoke with anguish in his voice. "Could a writer's block be the dragon's influence?"

"Yes! Since I used the magic to come to you and have since become your muse the dragon has reversed the spell and targeted you. We need to vanquish the dragon."

"Just like St. George and the dragon? I know the myth. I suppose you are the princess who is ensnared by the dragon through your magic. I will need a spear to thrust into the dragon," Garrett said, puffing out his chest.

"The dragon's lair is up in the highlands, in the mountain called Ben Nevis. We will need to start tomorrow after I bring the Spirit Spear, which was used to push the dragon into his present prison. The Spirit Spear has been spellbound to deal with the dragon. It has high magic to deal with the dragon because dragons are also magical beasts, which is why he was able to stop your creativity." Agnes started to get dressed. "I need to let the other Druids know what is happening. They will lend their magic."

"What should I do?" asked Garrett.

"Stay here and maybe do some research on how to destroy dragons."

Agnes leaned in and kissed Garrett. She left quickly.

Garrett knew Agnes was right, so he fired up his laptop and started accessing the internet on all subjects dealing with dragons. After four hours of cruising the internet, and slicing through the fantasy elements, some facts were found. The dragon's hide is incredibly thick and impenetrable except for their underside. To take care of this one flaw in their dreadful but beautiful bodies, the dragons coated their bellies with jewels and coins from the hoards they have. The dragon's treasure was from the populace who paid to keep the dragons from killing them or setting their crops to flames.

Presently Agnes returned. She had on

different clothing, a long, resplendent, shimmering silk gown of iridescent white and a heavily embroidered with magical symbols black wool cloak that looked very warm. She looked striking in the black and white uniform. She had mistletoe wound through her upswept hair. The whole picture of her was one of quiet Druid authority. "Have you done your research? Do you have a battle plan?"

Garrett nodded. "I know dragons have only their undersides being their weakness, flashing the only place to pierce. But they lay on their hordes to press into place metals and jewels to cover up their soft underbellies. Did the Druids put the dragon in his lair or another cave?"

"Another cave, I know because they

redistributed his horde."

"Good. We will have the element of surprise then because he will not think we're coming after him. I'm pretty fit from hiking in the highland hills and lifting my hand weights." Garrett sighed. "Let's get in a good night's sleep and tackle the dragon in the morning."

"We need to perform a Druid's blessing on this endeavour which involves the sacrifice of a lamb. I've got the lamb outside. Then after we sacrifice it, we need to roast the meat and eat it for our evening meal. Then we complete the ceremony by making love to bless the spell." Agnes then turned, brought the lamb inside. She dropped her cloak, divested herself of the glorious silk gown, and revealed her nude body painted with esoteric Celtic symbols in blue woad. The picture she presented was ferocious and erotic. She brought out a ceremonial knife with a bone haft and slit the lamb's throat with shocking violence. Catching the blood in a ceremonial dish she bled the lamb until it expired.

Then she lifted the dish to her lips and drained the contents, pausing then to look at Garrett with passion-filled eyes. Garrett was surprisingly turned on by her actions not aware of the magic that was swirling about the room which only enhanced the erotic atmosphere. Agnes turned to the lamb to start butchering it for their ceremonial dinner. Something about her cutting up the carcass nude festooned with painted symbols and muttering spells in

Gaelic as she did so mesmerised Garrett. Soon she had all the meat roasting. She turned to Garrett then beckoned him to follow her to the bed. He willingly followed her, and they sealed the spell with lovemaking.

***

At dawn the next day, they set out to slay the dragon. Garrett in black hiking clothes and Agnes in her white silk gown and heavy black cloak, she redid the runes in woad before leaving the house. They hiked up to the mountain Ben Nevis, reaching it nearly at noon. Agnes pulled out some cold lamb for them to eat. Once fortified they moved to the entrance. Agnes muttered in Gaelic some incantations to enter. They went in.

Once inside the darkness unnaturally surrounded them. Garrett got out his flashlight and lit it, reducing them to a small cone of light facing forward, the only lights coming from the beam and a curious glow from the Spirit Spear. The floor was sandy and the walls smooth. As they moved forward a deep, dark, sonorous voice surrounded them saying, "I know why you are here. I will not give up my millennium life easily. Writer, what makes you think you can win? You aren't a warrior. Druid, do you have enough magic to best me? You are alone and are only a new Druid. It took twenty Druids to place me here. I think not on both of your counts."

"Dragon, stop playing! You must be afraid of us to start a conquest by parsing out insults. Prepare to meet your end." Agnes then moved her hands in esoteric motions that elicited growls from the dragon as the binding hex found its place. "Quick, Garrett, move now to pierce him with the Spirit Spear!"

Garrett sprinted forward with the glowing Spirit Spear to find himself confronted by a two-story-high red dragon whose front arms were bound by a glowing blue rope, the back two limbs were also bound, rendering him secured tight. The dragon fought the ropes but to no avail, and he trumpeted his anger. Sitting up as he was, he exposed his soft underside, but

Garrett was horrified to see the dragon had covered his belly and chest with rocks leaving it impenetrable.

"You see Writer, I've left nothing up to chance. You have no place to use the Spirit Spear. But if you release me, I can challenge you to a duel of mind," growled the dragon.

"Don't accept the challenge! Dragons are devious and will talk you out of your soul." Agnes anxiously said.

"I am not without intelligence, Agnes. However, the dragon has covered his underbelly with the rock. There is no place I can pierce his hide with the spear. If accepting the challenge will give us a chance, then I will do it," Garrett authoritatively said. Agnes gasped knowing that only bad could come of this. Garrett turned to the dragon. "What sort of contest will this be?"

"The contest is to answer a simple word riddle, an answer a writer should have no problem providing one," the dragon intoned.

Garrett turned to Agnes. "I should be able to do this. Riddles are something I have experience with. In college, I was a member of a medieval club, and we would start our meetings with a riddle. I got very good at guessing them."

"Well, alright then but be careful, dragons are sly."

"Done then! Should you win, I will go back to sleep. However, if I win, I get the Druid to immolate as a human sacrifice."

Both Garrett and Agnes yelled out "No!"

But a high, female, disembodied voice chanted, "It is a binding contract!" Cackles were heard in the distance.

The dragon preened. "I will ask one riddle:

"Some try to hide, some try to cheat,

"but time will show, we always will meet.

"Try as you might, to guess my name,

"I promise you'll know when you I do claim.

"Who am I?"

Garrett looked at the floor, then up at the ceiling. "Some try to hide, some try to cheat, but time will show, we always will meet...hmm." He turned and looked at

Agnes. She looked at him with urgent regard, knowing that his answer is correct, would save her, and put the dragon back to sleep. But if wrong, she'd die a horrific death. Garrett felt the pressure. He knew the answer had something to do with the nature of an event in a person's life which couldn't be escaped, but that everyone feared. Then he thought he had the answer.

Clearing his throat, he stepped forward and looked at the dragon. "The answer is Age. Man does not like it and tries to cheat it, but age will always show up and take its toll." Agnes was hopeful. It was a brilliant answer.

The dragon laughed and rose to his full height, spread his wings, bursting the bonds on his feet. "Good answer well thought out. But it is wrong. The correct answer is Death."

Agnes gave out an anguished cry, and Garrett grabbed her in absolute passion. "Take me, not Agnes! I was the one to answer the riddle!"

"No, Agnes will pay as a Druid who cast the spell to put me to sleep the first time." With that the dragon let forth a jet of hideous flame. Agnes pushed Garrett away as hard as she could to save him. Then the dragon mercilessly immolated her. Agnes shrieked her pain then stopped and was quickly reduced to ash. Agnes was no more. Garrett, crying, got up to gather her ashes which he put in all his pockets.

"Go, leave this place. Your writer's block is no more, but with your newfound gift of writing, I curse you to not enjoy your wealth and fame. You will not be able to live with the guilt of killing the Druid," the dragon said. He looked at Garrett, then exited the cave, spreading his wings to go out in the world at twilight.

***

Garrett returned to his desolate cottage in the highlands. He got a jar for Agnes's ashes and put her on the kitchen table. He opened his laptop and retold this tragic, fantastic tale. He wrote straight through the night and all the next day. When he had finally finished, he sent it into his publisher.

His publisher was surprised but accepted the new manuscript. They printed it, and it quickly became a blockbuster making Garrett Jensen a rich and famous author. But he was unhappy. Garrett remembered from the research he did on dragons that they were intrinsically evil. Any agreement entered into with them will curse the participants tenfold. He was living proof. The dragon cursed him with a bestselling novel as he wanted but cursed him by not being able to revel in his newfound wealth because of the guilt he felt at Agnes's death. The dragon took away his love, Agnes, leaving Garrett alone. Garrett vowed to live forever like a hermit thereafter in the small, highlands cottage mourning his Agnes.

Then life reared its ugly head, an enterprising journalist wanted to interview this elusive writer that lived in a one-room cottage eschewing his wealth. Garrett Jensen had become even more famous because of his monastic lifestyle. The journalist after multiple attempts finally cajoled Garrett into an interview and set it up for that same day.

"Why didn't you spend your royalties from your book? It was a best-seller," The journalist asked.

The journalist was unpleasantly surprised to see Garrett looking at him with anguish in his eyes. Garrett whispered, "I can't enjoy the money. Because of me, my love, Agnes, died. I feel great guilt so I am unable to revel in my wealth as a dragon would," he said cryptically. "This is Agnes's song."

FINAL FAREWELL

By Zoey Xolton

Michael took a deep breath. A hundred lifetimes had passed since he'd killed her, and still his heart ached. He'd only been a new vampire then, not yet in control of the curse—the bloodlust—which afflicted his kind.

It was time. He wouldn't endure another night without her.

He just couldn't.

Throwing wide the castle doors, he met the sun with open arms. His golden hair caught fire, then his flesh blistered and peeled, before his entire form burst into flame.

As his damned soul burned, he saw her ghost—she beckoned to him.

"I forgive you, my love."

ABOUT THE PUBLISHER

BLACK HARE PRESS is a small, independent publisher based in Melbourne, Australia.

Founded in 2018, our aim has always been to champion emerging authors from all around the globe and offer opportunities for them to participate in speculative fiction and horror short story anthologies.

Connect

Website: *www.blackharepress.com*

Twitter: *@BlackHarePress*